That's What Friends Are For

VALERI GORBACHEV

PHILOMEL BOOKS · NEW YORK

For Kim Levich   —VG

PATRICIA LEE GAUCH, EDITOR

PHILOMEL BOOKS • A division of Penguin Young Readers Group • Published by The Penguin Group • Penguin Group (USA) Inc., 375 Hudson Street, New York, NY 10014, U.S.A. • Penguin Group (Canada), 10 Alcorn Avenue, Toronto, Ontario, Canada M4V 3B2 (a division of Pearson Penguin Canada Inc.) • Penguin Books Ltd, 80 Strand, London WC2R 0RL, England. • Penguin Ireland, 25 St. Stephen's Green, Dublin 2, Ireland (a division of Penguin Books Ltd.) • Penguin Books India Pvt Ltd, 11 Community Centre, Panchsheel Park, New Delhi - 110 017, India. • Penguin Group (NZ), Cnr Airborne and Rosedale Roads, Albany, Auckland, New Zealand (a division of Pearson New Zealand Ltd.) • Penguin Books (South Africa) (Pty) Ltd, 24 Sturdee Avenue, Rosebank, Johannesburg 2196, South Africa. • Penguin Books Ltd, Registered Offices: 80 Strand, London WC2R 0RL, England.

Library of Congress Cataloging-in-Publication Data   Gorbachev, Valeri. • That's what friends are for / Valeri Gorbachev. • p. cm. • Summary: When Goat finds his friend Pig crying, he imagines all the terrible things that might have happened to cause his distress. • [1. Crying–Fiction. 2. Friendship–Fiction. 3. Goats–Fiction. 4. Pigs–Fiction.] I. Title: That is what friends are for. II. Title. • PZ7.G6475Th 2005 • [E]–dc22 • 2004018118 • ISBN 0-399-23966-9 • 10 9 8 7 6 5 4 3 2 1
First Impression

It was a nice Sunday morning. Goat woke up in a
very good mood. His best friend Pig had invited
him to dinner.

"I wonder if my friend Pig has woken up yet,"
said Goat.

"Oh, no!" exclaimed Goat. He saw his friend Pig through the window. Friend Pig was in tears!

"Oh, dear," said Goat. "What could have happened to my friend Pig?"

Maybe one of the neighbors' boys trampled down Pig's favorite flowers, Goat was thinking.

Or maybe my friend fell down the stairs,
and is now in pain, Goat was thinking.

Or maybe he forgot to turn off the faucet in his bathroom! Goat was still thinking.

"Or maybe he forgot to turn off the iron and he burned his favorite shirt!" Goat was mumbling.

"Or he baked an apple pie for our dinner and robbers took it from him," Goat was whispering.

Goat ran to the window. "Don't cry, my friend," he shouted.

"I'll bring you fresh flowers from my flower garden.

"If you have broken your leg, Friend Pig, I will play chess with you every day to make you forget the pain.

"If you have flooded your house, I will help mop.
Count on me.

"If you have burned your shirt, I will bring you
my new shirt to wear. Don't worry.

"And if robbers stole your apple pie, I will make a new cabbage pie for our dinner. Never fear."

It was only late afternoon, but Goat couldn't wait a minute longer. He ran out of the house to Pig's house, carrying flowers, a chess game, a mop, a new shirt, and a cabbage pie in his hands.

"Hello, Friend Goat," said Pig through his tears. "You are early! I am still making dinner.

"Will you help me cut more onions for my stew?"

"Sure," said Goat.

"That's what friends are for!"